I0539329

THE WEIGHT OF SHADOWS

Reflections from the Edge

Book I of The Weight Trilogy

By

Chetan Rao

Copyright Page

© 2025 Chetan Rao. All rights reserved.
On the M.A.R.C. Publishers (www.onthemarcpub.com)

First Edition, 2025

The Weight of Shadows – Reflections from the Edge
ISBN: 979-8-9936911-0-7
Cover design by the author
Printed in the United States of America

Dedication

For all the strong women
who have helped shape me—
Your strength, grace,
and wisdom are the foundation
beneath every step I take.

FOREWORD

It is in the little things we see it.
The child's first step, awesome as
a supernova—Are you the new
person drawn toward me?
To begin with, take warning:
I am surely far different from what you
understand. Do you think I am
trustworthy and faithful?
Under God, we shall have new liberty.
Rising from ash
Happy, joyous, free.

by Michael F. Marcotte

PROLOGUE

"The story isn't of perfection, but of presence."

This is a story of cycles — beginnings and endings, of silence and noise, of absence and unexpected grace. It is the story of a boy from Bhopal who grew up believing that success could be measured in marks and accolades, but never in the quiet spaces within the heart.

It is a story of loss — of a father, of certainty, of self — and of the long, unrelenting journey to inhabit life fully, even with grief as a constant companion. It is a story of strength — of a mother.

It is a story of love — not as sentiment, but as a lifeline: a wife steady as a lighthouse, daughters whose affection becomes compass, friendships spanning decades and continents. It is also a story of service — of mentoring, of learning that the true currency of life is the change we help create in others, and in ourselves.

This story crosses continents: from India to the American Midwest, from university classrooms to service-driven organizations, into the spiritual landscapes of Nepal. It is a story of breakdowns and breakthroughs, of the black dog that lurks in shadowed corners, and of the quiet illumination that follows when one chooses recovery, presence, and love.

It is not a guide, nor a manual for living. It is a reflection — of mistakes, of courage, of small victories that often go unnoticed, and of the profound, invisible work of reclaiming a soul.

Ultimately, it is a story of transformation — of learning that joy is not in achievement, success not in accolades, and that the fullness of life begins only when one chooses to show up: for oneself, for others, for the world.

CHAPTER 1
OUROBOROS

*"Cycles end, begin, and leave
a quiet space for growth."*

Mike Thomas. A name that had slept in the corners of memory for three decades. A neighborhood kid who had somehow made it big in the land of plenty.

Karan hadn't thought of Mike since childhood — not until a WhatsApp call in March 2021 lit up his screen.

Mike Thomas. Who would have thought?

The Thomases were the only Christian family in Karan's predominantly Hindu neighborhood growing up in Bhopal. Somehow, Mike had learned that Karan would be in Dallas, probably through the spiderweb of social media, and wanted him to stay for a few days.

Karan reluctantly agreed.

Flying was easy for him now. He slept. His wife, Diana, teased that sleeping, cigars, and golf were his three hobbies. At forty-five, Karan felt, finally, that the war inside him had quieted. Flying was easy again.

Driving from the Dallas Fort Worth rental car garage to Mike's house, he drifted into memory. The monsoon had turned Bhopal into a city of puddles and mud rivers. *We were kings of small kingdoms, armed with nothing but stones and reckless joy.*

8

He bent low, measured his throw like an archer, and let the pebble skip once… twice… until it struck Mike Thomas squarely on the corner of his right eye. Blood spurted in slow, shocking arcs. The laughter of his friends died instantly.

Karan didn't wait to see if Mike's eye survived. He bolted — legs slick with mud, heart drumming in panic. He dove under the bed, panting, waiting for Baba's (Father) returning footsteps. The silence between the screams was the longest sound he had ever heard.

Decades later, driving through Dallas, Karan felt the same tightness in his chest. Hands slick with sweat, he pulled over, breathing deep — ten deliberate breaths, the way Tina, his therapist, had taught him.

Control returned, inch by inch.

That day in Bhopal, Baba's hand had found his ear — not cruel, just certain. Together they had walked through the rain toward the Thomases' home. Karan rehearsed his apology, voice trembling, words sticking like stones in his throat.

Mike's mother opened the door, her face a mixture of alarm and disappointment.

"I'm sorry," Karan whispered. "I didn't mean it."

The words felt enormous, alien.

Decades later, he sat across from Mike in a Dallas coffee shop smelling faintly of cinnamon and roasted beans. Mike's laugh still had that same clarity.

"You nearly put my right eye out," he said, grinning.

Karan laughed too — a little embarrassed, a little amazed.

The pebble that had once felt like a curse now felt like a circle closing.

They walked, talked, and forgave without ceremony. No grand gestures — just laughter shared across a table. Karan realized forgiveness doesn't always come wrapped in tears or rituals. Sometimes it arrives quietly, like a pebble returning home — *the tail of the ouroboros meeting its mouth, a cycle quietly renewed.*

CHAPTER 2
THE SWARM

*"Some mornings, the world shifts
while you bow to routine."*

11

Tuesday. Fresh water collection day — fifteen minutes from 2:30 to 2:45 p.m. Karan's backyard tank made them lucky; kilometers of rationed petrol and kerosene lines marked life in early 1980s Bhopal.

Karan woke up early. Twenty-five suryanamaskars (sun salutations), morning prayers murmured like protective incantations. And then, beyond the skyline, something moved.

At first, a swarm of insects. But closer they got, the shapes sharpened. Human faces — men, women, children — fleeing, herding, running as one trembling organism.

An hour passed. The sun climbed higher; his routine remained unfinished. Schoolwork waited, prayers unfinished, yet beneath it, a cold awareness settled: life could fracture in ways no ritual could prevent.

Downstairs, Aaji (grandmother) whispered her sacred readings. Baba (father) was away. Aai (mother) and Tai (sister) slept, untouched by the city's growing panic. Karan returned to his books, pretending the terraces and streets above were distant motion.

Days later, chaos unfolded. The Union Carbide plant downtown released a deadly cloud. Thousands died instantly; hundreds of thousands more suffered invisible, lifelong wounds. School vanished. Exams lost meaning. Life had changed forever.

Yet somewhere beneath the fear, a lesson took root: *survival begins in ordinary moments — a prayer, a breath, a quiet presence.* Later, far from Bhopal, this understanding would guide him through hairnets, pepperoni racks, and the humility of real-world lessons, where theory mattered less than patience, practice, and presence.

CHAPTER 3
FOUR DEGREES AND A HAIRNET

"The universe laughs gently at the gap between expectation and reality."

Karan adjusted the hairnet beneath his helmet for the third time, squinting under the fluorescent lights that bounced off rows of stainless steel machinery. The smell of drying pepperoni hung thick in the air.

Four degrees. From some of the best schools in the world.

And here he was — in Austin, Minnesota — bending over racks of pepperoni, trying not to look out of place.

His reflection in the steel panel was absurd: helmet perched like a crown, oversized coat flapping, eyes wide like a student caught cheating on an exam he'd already aced.

A supervisor approached. Clipboard in hand. "You new here?"

Karan nodded.

"Well, follow my lead," the man said. "You'll get the hang of it."

And in that moment, Karan realized — no number of degrees mattered here. Only the ability to handle a greasy rack without catastrophe.

He smiled faintly. *If only my thesis on protein–lipid interactions could prevent mold on hanging pepperoni.*

The next hour was a blur of noise, movement, and humility. When his clumsy hands faltered, a colleague caught his wrist. "See? Just like that."

Simple lessons from unexpected teachers.

During a break, leaning against a cold counter, Karan's thoughts drifted back to Bhopal — nights of chai and paper, his mother's soft footsteps, the glow of the desk lamp. Success had once meant marks, medals, perfection. Now it meant not dropping a rack.

By afternoon, he found rhythm. Laughter. Ease.

Even managed a joke: "My PhD finally prepared me for this."

The laughter that followed was warm, grounding.

Stepping outside, hairnet forgotten, Karan felt the cool Minnesota air hit his face.

Four degrees, a lifetime of theory, and yet — today's greatest lesson had come from a grinder and a rack of pepperoni.

Maybe this is what gratitude feels like, he thought.

Maybe humility was always waiting for me under a hairnet.

He smiled — and for a fleeting second, it felt as though the universe smiled

back.

CHAPTER 4
SNOW LESSONS

*"Humility arrives not in triumph,
but in the quiet thud of a fall — and
the laughter that follows when you
rise again."*

Karan stepped onto the icy sidewalk, boots squeaking like angry mice. Snow crunched underfoot, cold air biting his cheeks and turning his nose bright red. He had grown up in Bhopal, where winter meant a damp drizzle and mornings wrapped in a thin sweater.

And now, here he was in Madison, Wisconsin, navigating a world where the ground threatened to throw him on his face with every step.

His friend, Sean, walking ahead, laughed — a sound that made him both self-conscious and warm, despite the frost. Apparently, snow has a sense of humor, and it reserves its best tricks for newcomers.

He tried to imitate Sean, lifting his legs carefully and attempting a smooth glide, but the ice had other plans. His right foot shot out, sending him sprawling into a fresh pile of powder. Snow clung to his hair, jacket, and gloves, dripping slowly into his boots.

Sean's laughter rang through the air, half mockery, half delight.

Karan groaned, brushing snow from his sleeve. "How do you make this look so easy?" he muttered, his words muffled by the scarf wrapped around his face.

In Karan's mind, Baba's voice cut through the cold: "Don't fight the universe, Karan. Respect it. Learn from it."

Karan looked up. Imaginary Baba's eyes twinkled with a mix of amusement and patience.

"You see," he added, "nature doesn't care about your degrees, your smarts, or how fast you can read a textbook. It only cares that you pay attention."

By the time he reached the top of the small hill, sled in hand, he had fallen three more times, each time more gracefully than the last. His gloves were soaked, his boots heavy with snow, but a grin spread across his face.

He glanced at Sean, who was already sliding down effortlessly, and felt a small surge of pride. Maybe not a big achievement — no accolades, no certificates — but a personal victory nonetheless.

That night, as he watched the snow settle outside his apartment window, Karan realized humility isn't learned by reading about gravity — it's learned by slipping on ice, by surrendering to balance rather than conquering it.

By the time the snow melted, he was ready to move again — not away from failure, but toward the quiet rhythm of change.

CHAPTER 5
THE HOLE

*"Before ambition, before escape, there
was the quiet ache of wanting to
be seen – and the hollow that
taught him how to look with."*

Long before the snow, before Madison or Austin, there was Bhopal — hot, noisy, full of restless dreams and small humiliations.

Dust on his hands. Crickets loud. Smell from the eucalyptus trees. Heat sticky. Narrow streets of Bhopal, sun-bleached and dusty, smelling of wet earth after a sprinkle. Karan walking through a swarm of friends. Laughter bouncing off walls. Still alone.

Aunts comparing cousins. Cousins in America, cousins with accolades, cousins with everything that Karan didn't have. Small nods of approval. Fleeting praise. Temporary. Hollow. Always hollow.

"Why not me?" whispers in the skull, echoing louder than any cheer. Invisible rules, arbitrary universe, he doesn't know them yet.

Skipping school. Running down alleys, heart hammering, shoes kicking dust. Mischievous grin masking unease. Friendships fleeting. Laughter is loud. Inside, the hole yawns.

Mr. Patole sees him one afternoon. "Focus, Karan. Books. Numbers. There's a path out," he says. Calm, patient. Lighthouse in the fog. Karan nods. The world outside is unpredictable. Numbers can be tamed.

Exams. Papers. Study nights. Desk lamp flickers. Pages rustle like wind in trees. Bhopal smells of chai, dust, wet concrete. The Hole remains.

Evenings: terrace. Moonlight and shadows. Crickets slow. Friends gone. Alone. Dreaming of flights he has not taken. Places he may never see. The universe seems amused.

Small rebellions. Skipping class. Climbing walls. Kicking stones. Laughter with peers. Discipline a temporary balm. The Hole persists.

Visits to aunts and cousins in Belgaum. Comparisons sharp, unrelenting. "Why not you?" internal echo. The Hole stretches, deeper. Wants more than accolades. Wants recognition that feels like love, not numbers.

Roorkee entrance #89. IIT(Indian Institute of Technology) JEE all India rank #434. Numbers carved into memory, into pride.Moments of elation. Scores, ranks, congratulations. The Universe nods briefly. Chest rises. Emptiness returns. Satisfaction, like a mirage.

Even best friends cannot bridge it. Loneliness threaded through conversations, jokes, study sessions. The Hole grows quieter when ignored, louder when celebrated.

Night descends. Streets quiet except stray dogs, distant traffic, murmurs of cicadas. Black dog stretches along the spine. Waiting. Depression? Yes. Hollow? Certainly.

He wonders: will it ever fill? Will the universe ever hand him what he cannot take himself? Stars over Bhopal flicker, indifferent. Hole whispers: "Find meaning. Hurry. It waits for no one."

Karan curls on the terrace, notebook open, pen idle. Writes nothing. Thinks everything. The world is full of rules, successes, failures, comparisons. External validation abundant. Interior untouched.

Dreams: flight, distant cities, applause that never reaches the empty chamber inside. Tomorrow: study. Compete. Seek. The Hole persists.

CHAPTER 6
HARMONY IN THE DARK

"Sometimes, stillness teaches more than words."

Winter break from the first year at IIT Bombay. Karan sat beside Grand Uncle Bhau-da on the Punjab Mail as it rattled and clattered through the darkened countryside. The cold wind seeped through the cracks in the carriage windows, carrying with it the distant scents of smoke, wet earth, and the faint tang of spices from stations passed. Each mile brought him closer to Bhopal — closer to a city teetering on the edge of something he could not yet name. India simmered on the gunpowder of communal tension, a fragile balance of Hindu and Muslim neighbors waiting for a spark.

And then the spark came.

Friends became foes. Neighbors became enemies. The streets themselves seemed to pulse with suspicion and fear. Neighborhood watch gangs, armed with homemade swords and machetes, prowled the lanes, vigilant and violent. And through it all, Advani's rath yatra passed, leaving a wake of carnage and shattered trust, like a procession of fire through the heart of the city. The rath (chariot) yatra (journey) designed to unite Hindus, ended up fracturing the nation.

26

Karan arrived home, chilled by the winter air and rattled by the tension in the streets. He climbed the stairs instinctively, seeking his own space, and stopped short. In the darkened upstairs bedroom sat the back-side neighbor's family — the Muslim family he had played cricket with, shared snacks with, laughed with — cowering in silence, their eyes wide, bodies tense.

Fear sharpened everything. Karan's pulse thundered in his ears. He ran down the stairs, landing in the living room, where Baba sat quietly, Bhau-da beside him, smiling softly as if the storm outside were nothing but a distant whisper. Aai, Aaji, and Tai moved calmly about their tasks, their ordinary actions a defiance of the chaos outside.

"Why are they upstairs?" Karan asked, voice trembling.

Baba's gaze met his, steady and unwavering. *"Where else will they be?"*

The answer, simple as a stone dropped into still water, rippled through Karan. Harmony did not always come from law or order. Sometimes it came from courage, from shelter, from the deliberate choice to protect

27

rather than fight. From love practiced in small, precise acts. Baba had made a sanctuary in the eye of the storm — a space where fear could exist, but not dictate action.

Karan watched the family, their shoulders still tense, their faces shadowed in the dim light. And slowly, a lesson settled deep within him: chaos could rage outside, and yet inside, there could be order. Violence could sweep through the streets, and yet a home could remain a refuge.

That winter, in the quiet company of family and strangers alike, Karan glimpsed something enduring: that harmony is not the absence of fear, but the choice to rise above it. That sometimes, courage whispers quietly, and teaches more than the loudest lessons ever could.

And as the train had carried him across the country, the walls of his home now carried him across the edge of childhood and into understanding — a bridge between innocence and the heavy lessons of life.

As he lay that night, listening to the city's uneasy breaths, Karan realized that the lessons of courage and quiet presence would follow him far beyond Bhopal — into the strange, humbling worlds that awaited him next.

CHAPTER 7
LIFE IS A LAYOVER IN THE UNIVERSE'S TRANSIT LOUNGE

*"Every departure is an echo of becoming —
a quiet reminder that to move
forward is to be remade, again and again."*

30

Karan had learned that every major change in his life began the same way —
with a bag slightly too heavy, a sky too wide, and a strange mixture of fear
and hunger curling in his stomach.

Each move felt like a small death followed by an awkward rebirth. He had
come to see them as seasons, or perhaps — as Baba might say — "the
universe rearranging furniture." Still, that first one hurt the most.

The morning he left Bhopal, Aai packed chapatis wrapped in yesterday's
newspaper. The paper's ink smudged onto the aluminum foil, leaving a ghost
of headlines about monsoon floods and cricket scores. Baba stood in the
courtyard, pretending to check the car's oil gauge.

Neither wanted to say goodbye first.

"Call from the hostel," Baba said finally, still crouched by the wheel. "Not
just letters."

Karan nodded, the words catching somewhere between his throat and chest.
He looked at the familiar Ashoka tree that shaded the front gate — his first
witness to scraped knees, teenage sulks, and countless exams.

He wanted to freeze that moment. He also wanted to run.

31

The train to Bombay took fourteen hours and forty-three minutes — time that stretched and folded in strange ways. Through the grimy window, the landscape changed from familiar red soil to endless grey concrete. Each passing town felt like a reminder that the boy who left home wasn't coming back quite the same.

Bombay felt like another planet — a lush green campus surrounded by lakes and glass towers. The students spoke in equations, and laughter was a luxury reserved for those who had already solved the problem set.

Karan tried to blend in, but the rhythm of the city overwhelmed him.

The first week, he got lost three times — once in the maze of lecture halls, twice in his own thoughts. He missed the smell of wet earth, the lazy afternoons of Bhopal, the familiar voices.

Here, ambition had a sound — the clicking of keyboards, the whirr of ceiling fans, the sigh of someone staying up another night.

But slowly, the noise became music. He learned to thrive on instant coffee and deadlines, on the peculiar joy of fixing something that didn't exist yesterday. His professors became both tormentors and prophets, teaching him that truth often arrived disguised as failure.

Late at night, when he walked to the edge of Vihar Lake, the water would mirror the stars so perfectly that he felt suspended between two skies.

That's when he first sensed it — that circular rhythm the universe seemed to favor. Beginnings dressed as endings. Departures pretending to be arrivals.

Madison began with silence. The kind of silence that pressed against your ears, too clean, too wide. At first, Karan mistook it for loneliness. Later, he realized it was the sound of a life resetting.

The air was crisp, the streets orderly, and even the snow seemed to fall with American discipline — each flake landing exactly where it was supposed to.

Austin was different — a town of honest work, quiet streets, and murals of smiling pigs. The first week, Karan learned humility, patience, and how to navigate a world where your degrees mattered less than your presence.

At night, standing under streetlights, snow falling softly, he realized that life's transitions weren't punishments or rewards — they were invitations. Change would come again. And for once, Karan was ready.

He was learning that every city, like every person, forgives you if you stay long enough.

CHAPTER 8
THE ARRIVAL OF AMBITION

*"Success measured in grades, yet
the soul remains ungraded."*

The crowded platform smelled of diesel and departure.

Bombay heat — humid, sticky — clung to Karan's shirt as he hauled heavy luggage through the crowd. The city blurred past train windows, a kaleidoscope of color and noise. IIT Bombay in Powai awaited: the beginning of a world that promised respect, challenge, and identity.

Hostel room: bunk bed squeaks, ceiling fan hums lazily. The scent of new books and wet uniforms. Roommates shouting down corridors, laughter bouncing off the walls. Karan watches, learning the rhythm of belonging without ever quite joining it.

First class: Physics 101. Equations, calculus, relativity, formulas. Superior peers, brilliant minds. Karan nods, scribbles, calculates. Top ten percent. Pride swells. The hole beneath grows quieter but never closes. Alienation persists — even here, among the country's brightest. Always observing, never immersed.

Hazing stories. Midnight chai. Debates under banyan trees about existence and purpose. Friends who become temporary siblings. The hole yawns wider; the universe seems amused.

Scholarships arrive — Purdue, University of Wisconsin-Madison, University of Minnesota-Twin Cities, University of Iowa. He lists them neatly on a paper, folds it once, smiles faintly. "Congratulations," the universe whispers, and the hollowness answers, "Now what?"

Savita. Four years older. IIT grad student. Divorced, pragmatic, laugh like sunlight over water. Walks by Vihar Lake, evenings of poetry and laughter. For a while, the hole softens — not gone, just hushed.

Final year — exams, projects, goodbyes. Dreams of distant campuses and foreign skies. Beneath it all, a faint hum of anxiety. The weight of leaving home, leaving family, perhaps leaving himself.

Airport: Bombay to Heathrow, then O'Hare.

Aai, Baba, Tai and uncle at the gate, words caught in their throats. Two bags — one with clothes, one with a pressure cooker. $150 in his pocket.

"Take care," Baba says. Aai's eyes shimmer.

The universe winks — slightly cruel.

O'Hare. Jet lag, sterile light. Van Galder bus to Madison. Everything foreign — even the air. The cold bites. The heart carries a familiar companion: the hole, patient and waiting.

36

CHAPTER 9
THE DEEP HOLE

*"Achievements cannot patch
the soul; only presence can."*

Eagle Heights apartment. A borrowed couch. Srini and family — warmth that feels unearned, yet healing. For the first time, Karan experiences love without transaction. It feels strange. Necessary. The hole softens, then yawns.

That first night, cold air leaks through a cracked window.

Tears come quietly.

Far from Bhopal, far from IIT, far from self. The universe waits, unblinking.

The Regent: cold apartment, thin mattress, wind howling outside. The silence of snow unnerves him. Independence tastes like freedom — and loneliness. He learns both are sides of the same coin.

Campus life unfolds: girls, alcohol, laughter, experiments in escape. Fleeting warmth. The black dog — depression — follows quietly. Academic brilliance masks internal erosion.

Advisor: Dr. Evert. Predatory, controlling. Visa as leverage. Power wrapped in politeness. Karan sees what others don't — or won't. Anger simmers beneath stillness.

Basketball injury. ACL tears, hospital smell, isolation. Dr. Evert's visits feel invasive. The hole darkens, deepens.

Savita calls — seeks closure he can't give. Breakup, clean and cold. Nights blur: alcohol, weekend hookups, noise. Grades remain perfect. The hole remains untouched.

Then Diana — a quiet, angelic surprise.

Library conversations, coffee steam, laughter that feels like home. Winter hikes, poetry in snow. Universe tilts, slightly kinder. Hope returns in whispers.

Switch to Dr. Sastry: brilliant, humane. Six papers, four years. Awards, recognition. The outer world applauds; the inner one yawns. Meaning, he learns, must be built — breath by breath.

Night in Eagle Heights. Tea in hand. Diana beside him. Wind against the glass.

The hole isn't gone — just gentled.

Karan exhales. For the first time, he's not running from it.

CHAPTER 10
THE DRIFTLESSS DINNER

"Belonging begins not in words, but in the quiet exchange of trust over shared air and frying oil."

May 2000. Wisconsin's Driftless region — land untouched by glaciers, a valley carved by patience rather than violence. The drive there feels like falling into a painting: green folds of earth, slow streams where trout flicker like quicksilver thoughts, and air that smells impossibly alive — equal parts lilac, grass, and a stubborn whiff of freshly spread manure.

Diana hums along to the radio, steering with one hand, her other hand casually resting on Karan's knee. He wishes he could absorb her calm through skin contact. Instead, his palms sweat, his shirt clings, and his mind loops in anxious reels.

He's never done this before.

Dinner with *her* family.

In the heart of America's dairyland.

Six cars already crowd the gravel driveway.

"Oh boy," he mutters, adjusting his collar for the fourth time. "Is this... everyone?"

"Just the immediate family," Diana says, smiling.

Immediate, apparently, meant *half of Richland County*.

41

A sharp scent hits him as soon as the car door opens — oil, hot and thick, spitting somewhere nearby. "Grandpa John," Diana explains, "is frying fish. He's an artist about it."

"Fish?" Karan says, relief flickering. "I can handle that."

He rehearses his plan: *Go to Grandpa John. Talk fish. Delay meeting the crowd.*

Grandpa John turns out to be a weathered man with skin like tree bark and eyes that have seen too many Wisconsin winters. His baseball cap reads "Lund Boats," and his grin is missing a few teeth but none of its warmth.

"You must be Karan," John says. "Ever fried walleye before?"

"Can't say I have," Karan replies, trying not to sound foreign to his own tongue.

John chuckles. "Well, you're about to learn somethin' better than school."

The two of them fall into rhythm — the hiss of oil, the smell of batter, the breeze tugging at paper plates. John talks about fishing the Kickapoo and the Baraboo, about smallmouth bass and the secret spots where trout hide — "where the temperature drops and the water bends just right."

Karan listens, absorbing each word like oxygen. He adds a few comments — mostly about how fish taste when cooked with turmeric and mustard oil. John laughs loud enough to startle a nearby crow.

When a new batch is ready, John wipes his hands on a towel. "Take over for a bit, professor," he says.

Karan blinks. "Me?"

"You're doin' fine. Keep the oil honest. Don't let it get too cocky."

Something shifts in that moment. Karan feels — unexpectedly — trusted.

Not as an outsider, not as "the guy Diana brought home," but simply as another pair of hands keeping the oil from burning.

An hour later, John and Karan walk inside together, carrying platters of golden fish. The kitchen bursts with laughter, the smell of butter and pie crust, the gentle chaos of love.

Pam greets him first — kind eyes, warm hug, no hesitation. "Welcome, Karan," she says, and it sounds like she means it.

Then Alex — the father, serious, firm handshake, voice steady as oak. "Glad you could make it, son."

43

Two grandmothers, Elaine and Aleta, appear from the dining room, offering hugs and stories that tumble over each other.

The dinner stretches long and easy — stories, laughter, gentle teasing. Karan relaxes, one layer at a time. Somewhere between the fried fish and the lemon pie, he stops feeling like he's being evaluated. He just *is*.

Later, driving back under a dome of quiet stars, Diana squeezes his hand. "Thank you," she says softly. "I think they like you."

Karan smiles, his chest light.

"For the first time," he says, "I think I like me too."

He leans over and kisses her cheek. The valley fades behind them — a small, perfect world that smells of earth, oil, and acceptance.

CHAPTER 11
THE NIGHT OF FIRE AND SILENCE

"The world doesn't end in thunder. It ends in a quiet hallway that smells faintly of antiseptic and jasmine."

Family arrives. Wedding preparations. Aai, Baba, Tai, and little Adi. Laughter fills the small Eagle Heights apartment — until the sirens.

It starts with a high-pitched alarm, slicing through sleep.

"Out! Everyone out!"

Tai grabs Adi. Diana holds the door. Neighbors gather in the courtyard, breath visible in the cold Wisconsin air.

Karan looks around.

No Aai. No Baba.

He runs back inside.

Halfway up the stairs — Aai holding Baba, helping him down. Baba's face pale, steps slow. They reach the courtyard. The alarm stops. Silence. Something irreversible has begun.

Morning brings unease. Baba insists he's just tired, but Karan sees the tremor in his hands. "We're going to the hospital," he says, voice harder than intended.

46

ER lights. Machines. Voices sharp and distant. "Multiple strokes," the doctor says. "We've done what we can."

Baba never returns home.

Days dissolve into beeps and whispered prayers.

Aai's mala (prayer string, similar to a rosary) clicking softly.

Tai murmuring mantras.

Diana crying quietly in the hallway.

Karan stands still, detached — as though life has turned black-and-white, the sound turned off.

They let him go one week before the wedding.

Cremation in Middleton: priest from Milwaukee, aunts from Ohio and South Carolina. Fire, chants, and the faint smell of sandalwood.

A crater opens inside him — too deep to close, too vast to name.

"Block it out," he tells himself.

"There's a wedding. A thesis. A job."

He does.

Or thinks he does.

Because the world doesn't end in thunder.

It ends quietly — in a hospital hallway that smells of antiseptic and jasmine.

And it begins again in the silence left behind.

In the weeks that follow, the honeymoon postponed, Karan speaks only through motion — planning, defending, performing. Action becomes anesthesia. The world calls it resilience. He knows it's *just* survival.

PhD defended. GPA 4.0. Three degrees. Six publications.

The universe winks:

"You have everything — yet nothing."

CHAPTER 12
THE GROCER'S AISLE

*"Sometimes the universe whispers
its cruelties through strangers."*

Austin, Minnesota. Population twenty-five thousand and a half, if you counted the unborn.

A meat-packing town — one main street, half-shuttered stores, and a Dairy Queen that looked like it had given up years ago.

Karan arrived with a PhD, a fellowship, and the woman he loved.

Diana's laugh could still melt through his bad days.

He told himself: *This is what stability feels like.*

Days settled into rhythm — postdoctoral research, frozen winters, small-town kindness edged with curiosity.

The Minnesota way: nice, polite, restrained, never too direct.

The first snow fell like a clean sheet over memory.

He shoveled the driveway with purpose. The black dog was quiet.

Until the grocery store.

Thursday evening. Fluorescent hum, aisles half-empty.

A little girl stood by the cereal boxes, tears trembling on her lashes. Lost.

50

Karan crouched, gentle voice — the one he used with nieces back home.

"Hey, are you looking for your mom?"

Before she could answer, a woman turned the corner.

"Emma!" she shouted, running up, eyes sharp.

Then to the child: "I told you not to talk to strangers."

Her glare shifted to Karan — assessing skin, accent not yet spoken.

"Don't talk to him. He only understands Mexican."

For a second, the world froze.

The words hung there, absurd and surgical.

Karan half-kneeling, hand still extended.

Fluorescent lights flickered. Air thinned.

Something ancient cracked.

No anger. No defense. Just a deep, hollow quiet.

He stood, nodded once, left his cart by the endcap display.

Outside, snow fell again — soft, unbothered by human smallness.

He sat in his car, watching flakes dissolve on the windshield.

For the first time since leaving India, he knew:

Degrees couldn't buy belonging.

He had crossed oceans, earned alphabets after his name —

and here he was, reduced to a *brown* silhouette mistaken for another kind of foreigner.

On the drive home, silence.

Diana asked if he was okay. He said yes.

They made dinner, watched television, smiled on cue.

That night he dreamed of Baba — sitting wordless in the courtyard in Bhopal.

A silence with texture.

A silence that could swallow entire lives.

52

Morning came. He went to work, submitted revisions, wrote recommendations.

He told himself: *This is how you move on — by continuing to move.*

But something had shifted. The hole had grown teeth.

The black dog lifted its head.

In the reflection of his lab monitor, he saw his own face —

blurred, foreign, and almost unrecognizable.

CHAPTER 13
THE HOUSE OF MEAT AND GRANTS

"The mind can chase brilliance;
the soul keeps score."

Two years in.

Two papers published.

A growing reputation in the brittle world of academic chemistry.

Enough to earn nods from the right professors.

Enough to make his advisor smile.

Karan's lab at the University of Minnesota was spotless — beakers lined like soldiers, whiteboards crowded with equations that promised meaning if you stared long enough.

He worked late, chasing precision, pretending perfection might fill the hollow he could not name.

But academia, he was learning, wasn't discovery — it was endurance and *grants*.

Grant writing: equal parts begging and theater.

Ideas mattered less than funding.

Truth mattered less than politics.

One evening, his mentor — tenure-safe, eyes tired — said,

"Karan, you're talented. But science doesn't reward purity. It rewards persistence."

Karan smiled the polite immigrant smile that said *thank you* while translating it to *sell your soul carefully.*

The hole pulsed.

Baba's absence echoed in the centrifuge hum.

The smell of solvents — *antiseptic grief.*

At home, Diana thrived.

She found her rhythm in Austin — new friends, warm laughter.

She was sunlight in the endless winter.

They spoke of buying a house.

She wanted a porch swing and a lemon tree that would never survive Minnesota cold.

He wanted stillness — a place where the black dog might finally sleep.

They found it: a mint-sided two-story on a quiet street.

First night — takeout on the floor, no furniture, only laughter.

He thought: *Maybe this is how life repairs itself — quietly, without ceremony.*

But disillusionment deepened.

One night, over tea, he said,

"I think I'm done chasing papers."

Diana looked up. "You mean academia?"

He nodded.

"What will you do instead?"

He laughed, brittle. "Maybe something practical. Maybe just… breathe."

Her boss, Peter, mentioned a nearby company — food products, of all things.

From chemical kinetics to sausage casings? Absurd.

Yet curiosity tugged.

He met Dave, a manager with rough hands and honest eyes.

No pretense. No jargon. Just work.

At the end of the interview, Dave said, "You'll get your hands dirty here. You okay with that?"

Karan smiled. "I think that's what I need."

And so, the *arc bent again*:

From equations to emulsions.

From grants to grinders.

From the ivory tower to the house of meat.

Driving home through falling snow, he thought of Baba — grief's half-life.

Of Diana — love as rope, fraying when pulled too tight.

And the black dog, somewhere behind, trotting patiently in the snow.

CHAPTER 14
THE WEIGHT OF ORDINARY JOY

"The world called it stability.
His soul called it sedation."

The plant smelled of smoke, spices, and ambition.

Machinery moved with a rhythm both hypnotic and brutal.

Karan, in a hard hat and lab coat, watched pepperoni swing from metal racks like wind chimes from another dimension.

He had arrived —

A job with benefits.

A title with *Senior Scientist.*

A mortgage, a badge, a team that called him "Doc."

Every immigrant story needed this chapter — the one where struggle becomes structure.

Except structure wasn't peace. It was containment.

He told himself he liked the work — the chemistry of flavor, the precision of preservation.

Some days, he really did.

There was satisfaction in tangibility: results you could touch, smell, taste.

No proposals, no politics — just process.

Diana flourished, radiant in her career.

Evenings smelled of cumin and conversation.

Friends came over with casseroles and Midwestern courtesy.

It felt almost cinematic.

Anya arrived on a Tuesday morning — seven and half pounds, furious, full of hair, and perfect.

Karan held her, something in his chest unclenching.

Love finally had a shape.

"Welcome, little one," he whispered.

For a while, life simplified.

Diapers, deadlines, dinners.

He enrolled in an MBA — night classes, employer-sponsored.

Told Diana it was for "career growth."

Truth: he needed to fill the quiet spaces where the black dog liked to sleep.

Years folded neatly.

Promotions came. Sales, general management, mergers & acquisition. And so did fatigue. The hole pulsating, stretching.

Mira arrived — all eyes, full of hair and softness.

Diana glowed. Karan felt lucky, blessed even.

But blessings can be heavy when you don't know how to hold them.

The hole inside him never vanished; it simply changed shape.

Now it hid behind spreadsheets and frequent-flyer miles.

He smiled more. Drank more. Slept less.

At work — decisive, charming.

At home — still, blank, quietly eroding.

When the MBA diploma arrived, framed and official, Diana kissed him.

"No more degrees!" she said.

He smiled, but where will he hide from the black dog.

He thought of Baba — of unfinished conversations.

Of Bhopal rain.

Of the boy who'd once thrown a stone and spent decades apologizing to the universe.

Success surrounded him — wife, daughters, a good job.

Yet the silence inside grew louder, more articulate.

Late one night, after the girls slept, Diana found him in the dark living room.

"What are you thinking?" she asked.

He hesitated. "Just… how strange it is. Everything I ever wanted, right here. And still, something absent."

She took his hand. "Maybe it's not missing," she said. "Maybe you just can't see it yet."

He wanted to believe her.

He really did.

But somewhere deep within, the black dog stirred again — patient, familiar,

waiting for the next opening.

CHAPTER 15
THE ART STANDING STILL

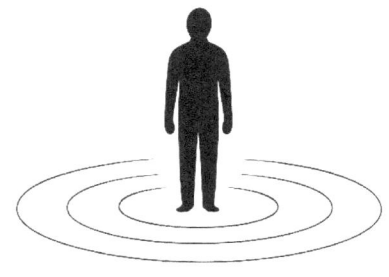

*"What you run from waits
for you in silence."*

The first tremor was subtle — a glass clinking against porcelain, almost rhythmic.

He told himself it was fatigue, too much coffee, not enough sleep.

But when he reached for a pen during a morning meeting and his fingers betrayed him, he felt something deeper stir — not fear, but recognition.

The black dog was awake again.

Diana noticed before he said anything.

"You're not sleeping," she said one night, eyes half-shadowed by the soft glow of the baby monitor.

"I'm fine," he lied.

They both knew it was a lie.

The air between them had become polite, efficient, professional — *colleagues on a shared project called marriage.*

Anya and Mira were asleep. The house hummed — a steady white noise of middle-class success.

A home paid for. A job secured. A family intact.

And yet, every night, Karan felt like he was moving underwater, through dense, invisible resistance.

He began walking again. Long, aimless walks through frozen streets.

Snow muffled the world, and for the first time in years, he could hear his own thoughts clearly enough to scare him.

He wondered if he owed himself the same — for ambition, for exile, for never learning how to just *be*.

At work, he stopped chasing promotions. He found comfort mentoring younger generation — reflections of the self he'd been before the hole took root.

One afternoon, during a meaningless strategy session, he caught his reflection in the glass window of the room.

Hair graying at the temples. Eyes softer, tired but alert.

He didn't look lost — just like a man who had finally stopped running.

At home, Diana asked if he'd thought about therapy.

He said yes — this time truthfully.

Tina — mid-fifties, unflappable, kind but unsparing.

She asked what he wanted.

"I want the noise to stop," he said.

She smiled. "Then stop trying to silence it. Just listen."

It sounded absurd, but something shifted.

Week by week, he stopped performing wellness and started practicing honesty.

Sometimes silence. Sometimes tears. Sometimes long drives with no destination, where sky and cornfields blurred into the same infinite color.

On one such drive, he pulled over on a dirt road outside Austin.

Sunset — pale orange dissolving into gray.

Cold air, distant geese, the smell of damp soil.

For once, he didn't reach for the radio or a distracting thought.

He just breathed.

A memory rose — Aai on the terrace, drying papads (similar to tortilla), humming.

Baba sitting quietly beside her, reading a paper he had read a dozen times.

They had known the art of stillness.

He never had — until now.

That night, beside Anya, helping her with a school project on constellations, he smiled.

"Did you know the universe expands?" she asked. "What does it expand into?"

"In itself, honey," he said. "*Like an ouroboros*, with its tail in its mouth."

Her small fingers traced lines between the stars, invisible threads across the dark canvas.

In that quiet moment — his daughter's breath steady, night calm — Karan finally understood:

Not every cycle ends with achievement.

Some end with presence.

He didn't need to chase the universe anymore.

He was already standing inside it.

CHAPTER 16
THE COLLAPSE

"Sometimes the soul must shatter
before it can let the light in."

The breakdown didn't arrive like thunder.

It arrived like frost — slowly, invisibly, everywhere at once.

On paper, Karan's life was flawless: a rising career, a loving wife, two daughters, a well-kept house.

Inside, something had gone still, even numb.

He woke tired, slept restless.

Laughter felt like memory rather than creation.

The black dog had grown bold again — padding behind him, breathing on his neck during meetings, curling up beside him when Diana slept.

There was no single moment of collapse, only a thousand tiny surrenders: another drink, a skipped meal, a morning pretending to be fine.

One day, the girls found him staring blankly at the kitchen wall.

"Daddoo?"

He blinked, forcing a smile that didn't fit.

"Just thinking, sweetie."

Work became both refuge and burden. Spreadsheets comforted — numbers didn't expect emotion.

He performed well; competence drowned despair.

But grief has memories.

The unwept tears for Baba had hardened into sediment, layers of unprocessed ache.

Even love struggled to reach him, though it tried.

It was Karan who called.

Ten days, the doctor said. A brief stay at Generose, Mayo Clinic.

The ward was ordinary, mercifully quiet.

No screaming, no padded walls. Just people sitting with books, puzzles, thoughts too heavy to carry alone.

He felt comforted and ashamed to belong.

The second night, he spoke.

"I shouldn't be here," he told a nurse.

She smiled — not kindly, not coldly. "Most people say that before they start healing."

Something broke — not collapse, but release.

Tears came without permission.

For Baba. For Aai's resilience. For Tai's support. For the versions of himself that had performed strength instead of seeking peace.

The hole didn't vanish. It simply stopped demanding to be hidden.

Diana visited nightly, luminous. Anya and Mira brought sketches — insisting Papa was *"in the hospital for superpowers."*

He laughed — clumsy, real, and for the first time in years, it didn't hurt.

Discharged, the world looked sharper. Colors richer. Silence, less menacing.

The black dog sat at a distance, watching.

On a work trip to Savannah, Georgia, life felt unmanageable. Invisible force dragging him to a local bar for a night of numbness.

The next day, he found himself at a local AA meeting — a church basement with metal chairs and burnt coffee.

"I'm Karan," he said. "And I'm... lost."

Heads nodded. No judgment. Just recognition.

Ninety days. Ninety meetings. Twenty-seven states. Church basements, community halls, dusty gyms.

Truckers, teachers, surgeons, poets — all searching for relief from themselves.

For the first time, he felt at home among strangers.

Sobriety was not a clean line — it was a trembling balance between falling and rising.

And slowly, something shifted.

He prayed — not to a deity, but to whatever force had kept him alive.

In that surrender, a small peace began — not loud, dramatic, just real.

On his first sober anniversary, he said to Diana,

"I think I've finally stopped running."

She smiled. "Then maybe now you can start living."

He nodded, unsure if she was right.

But deep inside, beneath scars and shadows, gratitude stirred — quiet,

patient, waiting.

CHAPTER 17
THE PILGRIMAGE

"Sometimes the mountain is not a destination, but a mirror."

Kathmandu greeted Karan with chaos and incense.

A blur of motorbikes, prayer flags, and dust.

The air smelled of smoke, spice, and devotion — the raw scent of life unfiltered.

He had come with no expectations.

Just over a year sober, he wanted only to see Aai — to sit beside her, to share silence without performance.

Aai was teaching in Pokhara now, a visiting professor among the foothills of the Himalayas.

Her letters had been steady and luminous — small anchors of calm during his unravelling.

Tran, his old roommate from Madison, had written out of the blue:

"I'll be in Hanoi, digging through archives. Could we meet in Nepal? Always wanted to see where the sky begins."

Karan smiled at the thought — Tran, the historian who found beauty in ruins.

They met in Kathmandu — two old souls, each with their own ghosts.

Tai and Bhau (her husband) arrived from India a day later.

The family together again, scattered pieces momentarily reassembled.

The streets pulsed with contradictions — monks scrolling on cell phones, beggars blessing strangers, temples echoing with chants that seemed older than language itself.

Here, Hindu gods and Buddhist saints shared the same skyline.

Every face seemed both weary and kind.

The drive to Pokhara was less a journey than an ordeal.

Narrow roads clinging to cliffs, switchbacks carved by rain and tremors.

The earth still bore scars from recent earthquakes — cracked bridges, half-fallen homes, and fields that looked freshly mourned.

In the backseat, Aai hummed an old Marathi lullaby.

Tran asked questions about faith.

Tai offered snacks.

Bhau, stoic as ever, gripped the wheel like a prayer bead.

And Karan, looking out the window, felt something loosen — a weight he hadn't realized he still carried.

When Pokhara appeared, nestled between lake and sky, it felt imagined.

The Himalayas stood in solemn grace, peaks brushed with light.

The air was clear enough to taste.

At night, stars crowded the horizon like whispered promises.

They visited Tibetan refugee settlements, where exile had become a community.

Children played near makeshift prayer wheels; elders spun them with fingers calloused by time.

At one monastery, a young monk invited them to stay for evening prayers.

Two hours passed like a lifetime.

Drums and deep chants filled the hall — vibrations that seemed to move through bone, not ear.

Karan closed his eyes. The sound rose, circled, entered him.

Then — a flash, not of sight but of understanding.

The feeling of being both infinitesimal and infinite.

Tears came, unprovoked. Not sorrow. Not joy. Just release.

After, he sat in the courtyard, breath visible in the cold.

Tran touched his shoulder, no words exchanged.

Across the yard, Aai smiled — she had seen the light in his face, the same one Baba once carried when he prayed.

In the days that followed, they visited shrines, temples, and lakes that mirrored the sky so perfectly it was hard to know where heaven began.

Karan walked slower, spoke less.

He didn't find answers — only better questions.

Was healing an ascent, or a return?

Did forgiveness require belief, or simply surrender?

As they prepared to leave, Aai said,

"Remember, beta (son)— mountains don't teach by speaking. They teach by standing still."

He nodded.

When the plane lifted from Pokhara, the peaks disappeared into clouds.

But the silence they left behind — that stayed.

Something in him had opened.

Not repaired, not resolved — just open.

And for the first time in years, the light entered without breaking him.

CHAPTER 18
THE QUIET REBUILD

"When the noise fades, even silence starts to hum with meaning."

83

Two years sober.

Karan measured time not in achievements, but in days that survived with grace.

Morning felt less like a battle, more like truce.

Life had texture again. Coffee tasted like something. The girls' laughter no longer came from another room.

Even silence — once threatening — began to sound like music learning its first notes.

Diana noticed first.

The tension that had sat between them, invisible but heavy, had softened.

She no longer watched him with quiet fear.

Now, their eyes met with gentleness — not forgiveness, not peace, but the slow rebuilding of both.

Inside, he reassembled himself — not quickly, not neatly, but truthfully.

His mind like a hard drive defragmenting after years of corrupted files.

Pieces of old faith, old pain, old meaning shuffled, reconnected in new ways.

The black dog still followed, but slower, hungrier only in absence.

Sometimes it slept for days; when it woke, he whispered, "Not today."

And most days, it listened.

He spoke differently now. Words like acceptance and grace felt natural.

He stopped trying to control the tides and started learning to float.

Not joy exactly — relief disguised as understanding.

The old job — proof of success — now tasted hollow.

Meetings about brand purpose and strategy left a metallic tang.

Food, once nourishment, had become data, propaganda dressed as sincerity.

At dawn, he wrote again — half-poems, half-prayers.

Fragments:

"The hole isn't a wound. It's a window."

"Maybe healing isn't fixing — maybe it's remembering."

Service whispered louder.

On weekends, he volunteered at a shelter.

The first ladle of soup into a stranger's bowl stilled something inside.

Not gratitude. Not pity. Recognition.

One evening, on the porch, Diana asked,

"You've been distant from work. What's going on?"

He exhaled. "I think I'm done pretending this means something."

She nodded. "You've carried that life long enough. Maybe it's time to carry something lighter."

He didn't reply. Didn't need to.

A month later, he resigned.

No drama. No farewell speech.

Just an email: "Grateful for the journey… time to begin again."

He accepted a role at a healthcare nonprofit, patient care at the center.

On his last night at the company, he stood alone, watching the highway hum past.

Flickers of past ambitions — beautiful, distant.

He whispered to the dark:

"Thank you for what you taught me. And for what you didn't."

Air cool, clean.

Somewhere behind the clouds, the universe exhaled — not applause, but quiet approval.

For the first time, Karan wasn't chasing meaning.

He was walking beside it.

CHAPTER 19
GRAVITY FAILS SOFTLY

"You can't fall off the earth
when you stop pretending to fly."

The first years at the nonprofit were a blur of light and exhaustion.

Airports, conferences, name tags, reports with words like *impact* and *innovation*.

Karan spoke in metrics, measured purpose in percentages.

Each success felt smaller than the last, each applause echoing faintly in a widening hollow.

The irony wasn't lost on him — *the man who once studied proteins and lipids now optimized "human outcomes."*

A different kind of chemistry, he thought. One with the same unstable bonds.

Diana thrived in her rhythm — work, children, community.

Her laughter had a clarity that made him ache.

She was steady; he was static.

He loved her deeply, from a distance, as though his restlessness might stain her light.

At night, he opened his laptop and scrolled through old research papers, wondering if his name still meant anything.

Sometimes he found it — buried in citations, a line of text proving he once mattered.

The comfort lasted five seconds.

The black dog slept lightly now.

He had learned its habits: when it would stir, when to feed it distractions — a project, a title, another cause to champion.

He was careful not to look it directly in the eye.

When promotions came, he smiled dutifully.

5 years sober.

When the team toasted him with champagne, he excused himself to "check email."

In truth, he went to the restroom, splashed cold water on his face, and stared at the man in the mirror — accomplished, respected, hollowed.

"Congratulations," he whispered. *"You've officially won the game you didn't want to play."*

That winter, during a leadership retreat in Scottsdale, a young colleague asked, "How do you stay so calm all the time?"

He almost laughed.

"Practice," he said.

What he didn't say: *numbness looks a lot like calm if you hold still long enough.*

6 Years sober. The arc of spiritual growth flattening out.

Weeks later, Diana found him in the garage, staring at an old pressure cooker from Bhopal — always unpacked, rarely used.

"You okay?"

"Just remembering," he said.

She waited. He didn't elaborate.

Memory had become his only form of prayer.

That spring, his doctor mentioned "elevated blood pressure."

Karan nodded. Made a note to "reduce stress."

But stress wasn't the disease; it was a disguise.

The hole had matured — no longer screaming, only humming, loudly.

A quiet, patient ache, like gravity reminding him that all things must fall, unless you are above it all.

One Sunday, while mowing the lawn, a wave of dizziness forced him to sit.

Suburban quiet dissolved — the smell of cut grass, sprinklers, children's laughter — blurred into one weightless hum.

He realized how little of his life he had truly lived.

That night, he dreamt of Baba.

Not frail, not dying.

Just sitting cross-legged in the courtyard, looking at him.

No words. Only a steady gaze.

When Karan woke, his pillow was damp. Sweat or tears — he didn't know.

The next morning, he drove to work but couldn't go inside.

He parked a few blocks away, whispered:

"I can't keep doing this."

He didn't mean work. He meant pretending the purpose could be outsourced.

That night, over dinner, he told Diana he wanted time off.

She didn't argue.

"You've been carrying the weight for a long time. Maybe it's time to set it down."

He nodded, grateful and terrified.

And just like that — the first crack appeared.

Not one that destroys, only one that lets light in.

CHAPTER 20
STILL WATER KNOWS

*"When you stop running, the
world starts walking toward you."*

The first day of stillness felt unbearable.

No meetings. No inbox. No charts or calendars to explain his worth.

Karan sat in the kitchen, watching coffee swirl, steam rising like a question he could finally hear.

He had promised Diana he wouldn't turn the break into another project. He didn't.

He just sat.

Weeks passed. Silence hurt more than exhaustion ever had.

He could hear everything — the clock ticking, furnace humming, the ache of unfilled hours.

The black dog paced at the edge of his thoughts, confused by the absence of chaos.

In the third week, he started walking.

No headphones, no podcasts. Just breath frosting in Minnesota air.

He passed the same mailbox, the same church, the same grocery store where, years ago, a mother had pulled her daughter from him.

This time, he didn't flinch.

He whispered, "It's okay." Not to her. Not to himself. *To the echo of a wound long denied rest.*

One morning, at a small frozen lake on the east edge of town, he stood listening to nothing.

And then something shifted.

Silence wasn't empty. It was full — of memory, loss, everything he had pushed away.

Baba — calm voice, quiet fixes.

Aai — letters in looping Marathi (Indian language), always ending: "Be good, beta (son)."

Tai — always supporting.

Diana and the girls — laughter, grace, living without proving anything.

Maybe this was grace. Not absence of pain, but permission to feel it without drowning.

He began reading again — not research papers, but philosophy, poetry, fragments of Upanishads.

Lines once dismissed now burned gently in his chest:

"The Self is not to be known by much learning, but by him whom It chooses — It reveals Itself."

For the first time in decades, Karan didn't want to understand the universe.

He wanted to belong to it.

Slowly, the rhythm of his days changed.

Morning walks, simple meals, evenings with Diana and the girls.

Conversations wandered without agenda.

He laughed more. Slept deeply. Dreamt less.

One night, at the kitchen window, watching snow drift under a streetlight, he realized —

the hole in his soul hadn't closed, but it no longer terrified him.

It was just space. Room for light to move through.

He whispered a quiet thank you — to Baba, to Aai, to Tai, to Diana, to the unseen architecture of mercy that had held him even when he refused to be held.

Still water knows, he thought.

It remembers every stone ever thrown, and yet it reflects the sky perfectly.

CHAPTER 21
SERVICE REDEFINED

*'When love becomes the currency,
work becomes devotion.'*

The phone vibrated on the kitchen counter — a polite ping, nothing urgent.

Karan glanced at it but didn't answer immediately.

Instead, he sat at the table, notebook open, blank pages waiting — as he had learned to wait for life itself.

Months of stillness had given him clarity.

The black dog lingered, but boundaries had been set.

He no longer tried to silence the hollow inside; he invited it to sit quietly, companion not predator.

One morning, reading about small businesses struggling during the pandemic, a thought struck him:

"What if... something could help them navigate better? Connect, organize, empower?"

Slowly, a concept took shape.

Not a company for accolades. Not a platform for money.

A bridge. A way for others to find their way, to find each other, to do work that mattered.

100

He built it methodically, drawing on every skill he had accumulated — finance, strategy, chemistry, research, analytics, problem-solving. *Most importantly, love as the currency.*

But this time, there was no pressure. No chasing recognition. No comparison.

It was a service. *Pure, intentional, and deliberate.*

A platform for small businesses to grow. A place where mentoring young entrepreneurs became natural, impact tangible and immediate.

He watched a high school student coordinate their first project.

Her smile — wide, triumphant, unguarded — felt like sunlight.

A follow-up platform came next. Sister projects, born from the same philosophy: empower, simplify, support. *Most importantly, love as the currency.*

Every event, donation, volunteer coordination became a ripple.

Currency wasn't money — it was trust, connection, love. *Karan finally bridged the chasm between the material and the spiritual currency.*

The energy, Karan had finally learned, could fill a void that degrees, jobs, and promotions never could.

He mentored young professionals in recovery, teaching not just skills, but principle: giving is receiving. Leading with empathy builds resilience. *Failure is a teacher, not a verdict.*

He traveled for purpose: workshops in small towns, talks in community centers, retreats for those finding sobriety, and back to India — Bhopal, Belgaum, Mumbai.

Under the shade of a jackfruit tree near his childhood home, he felt the same breeze Baba once did.

He remembered the little pebble, the apology, the lifelong chase for meaning.

Now, life had come full circle — not as achievement, but as service.

Diana watched him with quiet pride. Daughters thriving, home warm and alive.

Every day, he understood the paradox he had lived to solve:

Happiness isn't chased. It arrives when pursuit is released.

Impact isn't earned. It grows when love becomes currency.

The hole remained — crater, hollow space, reminder.

But it was fertile.

From it grew recovery, mentorship, connection, contribution.

Late at night, he would write emails to a businessman in Seoul, a CEO in São Paulo, a peer in Mumbai.

Replies would come: "Thank you. You showed me a way."

In that, he felt it — the quiet alchemy of service transforming pain into purpose.

The black dog sat quietly in the corner, watching. Content.

Because now Karan had learned the secret that had eluded him for decades:

Love, when used as currency, never runs out.

CHAPTER 22
RETURNING HOME, WITHIN AND WITHOUT

"You carry home inside you;
sometimes the journey is path
to seeing it."

Karan stepped off the plane in Bhopal.

The clean air hit him like a revelation — crisp, sharp, alive.

Years had passed, yet the smells, the sounds, the energy of India were immediate, unapologetic, humbling.

Diana's hand found his as they walked through the bustling streets — horns blaring, children darting, incense curling into the sky.

Anya and Mira clung to her, bright-eyed, curious, fearless.

Karan smiled. For the first time in a long time, he felt entirely present.

Bhopal, with its calm lakes and green landscape, became their sanctuary.

Early mornings brought meditation at sunrise. He learned to listen — not to the city, not to the crowd, not even to ambitions — but to the quiet beneath the noise, the pulse beneath grief, the rhythm beneath success.

He visited Aai and Tai. Time had etched lines into their faces, but eyes still held fire.

They spoke of parathas (flat bread), mango trees, cricket scores — mundane things that flowed with a deeper current: love, resilience, continuity.

Karan realized that meaning had not been lost. It had been waiting at home all along.

He met young entrepreneurs, scientists, students, and friends.

He shared stories — not of accomplishments, but of breakdowns, sobriety, and the winding path to self-compassion.

Love, he realized, was the currency of change. Knowledge was the tool. Presence was the act.

Every temple visit, sunrise, and quiet evening with Diana brought lessons:

- Recovery is not a finish line; it is a lifelong practice.
- Growth is not linear; it bends, doubles back, circles, sometimes leaps.
- The hole never fully disappears, but it can be held, observed, softened by love, service, and connection.

In the hills overlooking Belgaum, Karan watched mist settle over the lake.

He thought of the black dog and smiled. It was not an enemy, only a reminder of what mattered.

Grief and joy, loss and love, ambition and humility — all intertwined, inseparable.

Returning to Austin, Minnesota, the world felt different.

Streets, labs, meetings — he moved through them with quiet certainty.

Work and mentorship were no longer about achievement. They were about alignment: inner truth meeting outer action.

He didn't chase happiness. He cultivated presence.

He didn't seek recognition. He offered service.

He didn't hide the black dog. He walked alongside it.

And in doing so, he discovered: love — freely given, intentionally practiced, shared — was medicine for others and for himself.

That evening, sitting with Diana and the girls as the sun dipped behind cornfields, Karan realized:

He had come full circle.

Not by reaching a destination, but by embracing the journey — wholly, tenderly, courageously.

The hole remained, yes, but it no longer controlled him.

The black dog rested.

For the first time, Karan felt home — within, without, and everywhere in between.

CHAPTER 23
SERVICE AS PURPOSE

"Change begins not in wealth or acclaim, but in the courage to show up for others."

Karan's mornings began early.

Not with spreadsheets or emails, but with reflection — meditation, journaling, silent gratitude.

The black dog still lurked occasionally, but he no longer fed it with avoidance or alcohol.

He acknowledged it, then returned to action.

The platform he had built for small businesses had grown.

What started as a simple tool now transformed communities into global networks of support.

Every business, campaign, donor, and volunteer reminded Karan: real impact was relational. Human.

He taught not just finance, strategy, chemistry, biology, or marketing, but patience, empathy, and the courage to persist through the internal voids life sometimes carved.

Love became the currency — freely given, intentionally invested, multiplied through action.

He traveled yearly — to India, to U.S. conferences.

Everywhere, he listened. He learned. He shared stories of failures, breakdowns, and recovery.

He spoke of the black dog without fear, the hole without shame, and the way love, service, and presence could transform even the deepest pain into a platform for others.

In Austin, he and Diana hosted gatherings — for young families, newcomers, those struggling silently.

Anya and Mira learned that home was more than walls or furniture.

Home was care, attention, and courage to be fully human.

He watched them — laughter spilling freely, curiosity sharp, fearless — and understood: legacy was not money or awards. It was presence. Modeling life fully, shadows and light alike.

Late nights, after workshops or mentoring, Karan sometimes sat alone, looking out over cornfields or lakes.

The hole was smaller now. The black dog slept.

He felt gratitude — not only for what he achieved, but for what he survived, learned, and could offer.

The world still demanded, still misjudged, still overlooked.

But Karan no longer sought validation in its eyes.

He had learned the rhythm of giving, the power of listening, the joy in simply being present.

Life was not about filling the void, but about reaching out to others — creating bridges of love, mentorship, recovery.

Every life touched, every young mind inspired, every broken spirit uplifted — this was his measure.

This was his purpose.

He remembered Austin's grocery aisle, Bhopal's streets, labs and lectures, heartbreaks and breakthroughs.

Everything had led here: to service, to presence, to love as currency.

And in that quiet, ordinary, extraordinary moment, Karan understood: home — true home — was not a place, a degree, or a title.

112

It was the echo of care reverberating through lives he touched.

For him, that echo would never fade.

CHAPTER 24
FULL CIRCLE

*"The universe measures not
what we earn,
but what we return."*

Karan stood on the balcony of a small home in Belgaum.

The wind carried pine scents and the soft flutter of prayer flags.

Children laughed in the streets below, wide-eyed, lives untouched by burdens he had carried, focused on gully (side street) cricket.

For the first time in decades, he felt whole.

The black dog still existed — a shadow in the corner — but it no longer dictated terms.

It was a companion, a reminder of endurance, not a jailer of despair.

He thought of Bhopal: the monsoon, the pebble that had flown too far, Baba's silent wisdom.

All of it had led him here.

The company he started thrived — a platform for connection, mentoring, service.

A space where guidance and community met action.

Karan spent hours with young professionals, students, and those in recovery.

He shared lessons learned the hard way: love, patience, integrity, service — currencies far more enduring than money.

He reconnected with India — not in nostalgia, but in conscious engagement.

Visiting childhood streets, speaking to students, mentoring leaders, quietly contributing to communities that shaped him.

Rootedness that had eluded him for decades bloomed.

Back in Austin, Diana and the girls flourished.

Their laughter and warmth filled the house — testament to patience, love, resilience.

Karan watched, heart unburdened by the need to prove, measure, or chase.

The hole remained, but had become a vessel — space for joy, gratitude, purpose.

The black dog rested quietly.

He realized life's journey was never about perfection, accolades, or escaping grief.

It was about showing up — for oneself, family, strangers, communities.

Choosing transformation over comfort, service over accumulation, love as guide rather than reward.

The sun set over distant ridges.

Karan whispered a silent thanks:

For failures that became lessons.

For love that became light.

For life that became a bridge.

And in that moment, he understood fully:

The story never truly ends.

It evolves.

Cycles continue.

The hole remains, softened by grace.

The black dog sleeps.

And love — unmeasured, relentless, patient — carries him forward.

EPILOGUE
THE QUIET AFTERLIGHT

*"Every ending hums with
the echo of beginnings."*

Years later, the house in Austin hums differently. 9 years sober.

The girls are grown — their laughter less constant but more intentional, like music carried on the wind.

Diana still tends to her garden, talking to the basil and rosemary as if they are old friends.

Karan watches from the porch, coffee in hand, sunlight filtering through the oaks.

Life no longer demands explanation.

It simply *is*.

He thinks often of Baba — not as absence, but as presence diffused through memory.

In the way he folds his newspaper.

In the quiet pauses before answering a question.

In patience he has finally learned to offer others.

And Aai — the steady flame — still calls from Belgaum, her voice smaller with age but warmer than ever.

Tai — ever a supporting presence.

The old restlessness is gone.

The ache that once defined him has transformed into attention to the warmth of a hand, the taste of morning air, the sound of laughter returning down a hallway.

He writes sometimes now — not to be read, but to remember.

Small essays, reflections, fragments of grace.

On grief, on renewal, on the strange generosity of time.

When people ask what he's learned after all these years, Karan smiles.

"That we are all travelers," he says softly.

"We don't escape our shadows — we learn to walk with them."

The sky deepens to gold, then indigo.

The black dog stirs, stretches, and lies down again.

Somewhere, a child laughs — the same sound that began it all.

And in that sound — fleeting, luminous — The circle closes once more.

120

Foreword Contributor Tribute

Michael Frederick Marcotte

Michael Frederick Marcotte is a visionary aviator, rocket engineer, technology leader, cybersecurity pioneer, quantum physicist, and international security advisor. His life has bridged air, earth, and code — from launching satellites to shaping global cybersecurity, from quantum research to humanitarian service.

He served as President of Hughes and Global Chief Information Officer at EchoStar/DISH Network, and has held senior leadership roles in over seven global corporations. A co-founder of the United States National Cybersecurity Center (NCC) and founder of its National Rapid Response Center, Michael has devoted his career to the protection of people, systems, and truth.

Honored twice by NASA for engineering excellence and by the United States Air Force for his contributions to national defense, Michael remains guided not by acclaim but by purpose.

A son of the Colorado Rockies and a citizen of the world, he has touched nearly every chapter of modern innovation — the birth of the Internet, artificial intelligence, and the dream of space exploration — yet his defining legacy is one of generosity, mentorship, and light.

"If I am half the man Chet Rao is, then I will have been a good man."
— **Michael Frederick Marcotte**

Author Tribute

Chetan (Chet) Rao

Chetan (Chet) Rao is a scientist, investor, entrepreneur, mentor, inventor, and founder — a bridge between worlds of logic and light. His work moves through science, technology, and human understanding, grounded in the belief that invention gains its worth only when it serves compassion.

Educated at the University of Wisconsin, the University of Minnesota, and the Indian Institute of Technology Bombay, Chet has led and advised global organizations across healthcare and consumer innovation. His research and leadership reflect a lifelong pursuit of meaning — where systems meet stories, and where insight becomes empathy.

Beyond business, his work is an exploration — of memory, purpose, and the architecture of the human spirit. As a mentor and thinker, he is known for his quiet precision and his belief that progress without compassion is incomplete.

Through *The Weight Trilogy*, Chet explores that same boundary — between self and soul, certainty and surrender — tracing the unseen forces that connect creation, consciousness, and grace.

123

"Between knowing and understanding lies the weight of being."
— **Chetan Rao**